MAX & MO
Let's Make a Snowman!

For another set of best friends,
Max and Mia —P. L.

For Patricia Lakin,
with thanks —B.F.

ISBN-13: 978-0-545-12885-8
ISBN-10: 0-545-12885-4

12 11 10 9 8 7 6 5   9 10 11 12 13/0

PRINTED IN THE U.S.A.   40

FIRST SCHOLASTIC PRINTING, DECEMBER 2008

DESIGNED BY LISA VEGA

THE TEXT OF THIS BOOK WAS SET IN CENTURY OLDSTYLE BT.

MAX & MO
Let's Make a Snowman!

By Patricia Lakin
Illustrated by Brian Floca

Ready-to-Read
SCHOLASTIC INC.
New York Toronto London Auckland Sydney
Mexico City New Delhi Hong Kong Buenos Aires

Max and Mo were
best friends.
They loved to curl up
in their cozy cage . . .

. . . in the art room
to watch the big ones.

"What are they making?"
asked Max.

Mo read the sign.
"Snowflakes," he said.

"Like those?" Max pointed.

"SNOW!" the big ones cheered.
"Let's go outside!" said the
biggest one.
Hats and mittens flew.

Mo climbed up.

He pulled
Max up.

"Look!" said Max.

"They are making a snowman."

"We will make one too,"
said Mo.

"Go outside," said Mo.

"Too cold!" they said.

They ran back inside.

Max scratched his ear.
"Now what?" he asked.

Mo scratched his chin.

He saw a bin.

"Dive in!"

Paper and glue flew.

Cups, seeds, and yarn too.

"But we have no snow,"
said Max.

"We do not need snow,"
said Mo.
"We need white circles."

"Trace this!" said Max.

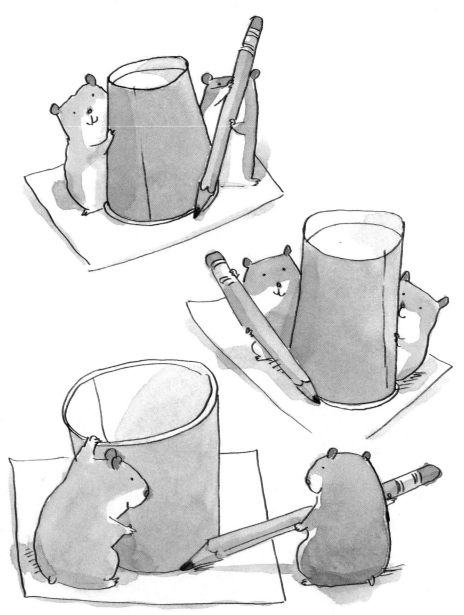

They made three circles.

They cut.

They taped.

"Look! said Max.

"Their snowman can stand up."

Mo scratched his chin.

They taped their circles to a tube.

"Now ours can too!"

"Look!" said Max.

"Their snowman can see
and smile."

Mo scratched his chin.

They glued
on seeds.

"Now ours can see
and smile!"

"And our snowman will get
a hat," said Mo.

"And a scarf!" said Max.

"And arms!" they said.

"We made a great snowman!"

Max and Mo curled up
with their snowman
in their warm, cozy cage.

Want to make a snowman?

Here is what you will need:

1. A grown-up's help
2. Paper
3. Scissors
4. Pencil
5. Tape
6. Paste
7. Seeds, raisins, or peppercorns
8. Yarn or ribbon
9. Two toothpicks
10. Cup
11. Black paint or marker
12. Egg carton
13. Paper towel tube
14. Ruler

Here is how:

1. Trace

2. Cut

3. Tape

4. Measure

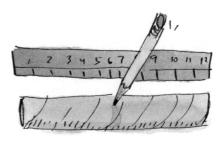

5. Cut

6. Tape

7. Paste

8. Cut

9. Paint

10. Paste

11. Tie

12. Tape